This book belongs to:

. . . .

. . . .

Retold by Sue Graves
Illustrated by Andrew Breakspeare

Reading consultants: Betty Root and Monica Hughes

Marks and Spencer p.l.c.
PO Box 3339
Chester, CH99 9QS

shop online
www.marksandspencer.com

ISBN 978-1-84461-587-2
Printed in China

First
Readers

Read Together

The Ugly Duckling

MARKS &
SPENCER

Helping your child to read

First Readers are closely linked to the National Curriculum. Their vocabulary has been carefully selected from the word lists recommended by the National Literacy Strategy.

Read the story

Read the story
to your child
a few times.

It was spring.
Mother Duck sat on her eggs.
She had six eggs in her nest.
The eggs began to hatch.
Out came five yellow ducklings.

8

Follow your finger

Run your finger under
the text as you read.
Your child will soon begin to
follow the words with you.

Look at the pictures

Talk about the pictures. They will
help your child to understand the story.

Mother Duck sat on her eggs.

9

Have a go

Let your child
have a go at
reading the large
type on each
right-hand page.
It repeats a line
from the story.

Join in

When your child is ready,
encourage them to join in with the
main story text. Shared reading is
the first step to reading alone.

It was spring.
Mother Duck sat on her eggs.
She had six eggs in her nest.
The eggs began to hatch.
Out came five yellow ducklings.

Mother Duck sat on her eggs.

Soon only the big egg was left.
Mother Duck sat back on her nest.
The big egg cracked.
Out came a big grey duckling.
"Look how ugly he is!" said the
other ducklings.

The big egg cracked.

Mother Duck took the ducklings to
the pond.
"Follow me," she said.
The ducklings all swam on the pond.

The ducklings all swam
on the pond.

Some wild ducks were on the pond.
They saw Mother Duck.
They saw the five yellow ducklings.
Then they saw the big grey duckling.
"Look how ugly he is!" said the
wild ducks.

"Look how ugly he is!"

The ugly duckling was sad.
"We will go to the farmyard," said
Mother Duck. "Follow me."
She took the ducklings to the
farmyard.

The ugly duckling was sad.

Some hens were in the farmyard.
They saw Mother Duck.
They saw the five yellow ducklings.
Then they saw the big grey duckling!
"Look how ugly he is!" said the hens.

"Look how ugly he is!"

The ugly duckling was sad.
"I am so ugly," he said. "I will
run away."
When Mother Duck was busy, the
ugly duckling ran away.
He ran far away from the farm.
He ran far away from the pond.

The ugly duckling ran away.

The ugly duckling came to a big lake.
He hid in the tall reeds.
He hid for a long time.
Soon it was winter.
It was very cold.
The lake turned to ice.

The lake turned to ice.

Then winter turned to spring.
It was warm again.
But the ugly duckling still hid in
the reeds.
Then, the swans flew by.
They saw the ugly duckling.
They flew down to him.

The swans flew by.

"How fine you look!" said the swans.
"But I am an ugly duckling!" he said.
"No you are not!" they said. "Look!"
The duckling looked in the water.
He was not an ugly duckling at all...
he was a swan!

He was a swan!

Look back in your book.
Can you read these words?

Mother Duck

egg

ducklings

pond

hens

swans

Can you answer these questions?

How many eggs were there?

Which animals were
in the farmyard?

What did the ugly duckling
change into?

Read Together

Look out for other books in the **First Readers** range (subject to availability):

Fairytale Readers

 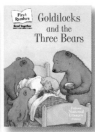  

Hansel and Gretel — Goldilocks and the Three Bears — Jack and the Beanstalk — Beauty and the Beast

The Enormous Turnip — The Elves and the Shoemaker — The Emperor's New Clothes — Cinderella

The Three Billy Goats Gruff — The Three Little Pigs — The Princess and the Pea